Y0-CAW-772

THIS BOOK
BELONGS TO

SPIRIT OF THE SAMURAI

OF SWORDS AND RINGS

Gary Reed
&
Rick Hoberg

When adventure is your destination!

Boston • Detroit • Phoenix • Seattle

Visit us online at www.actionopolis.com

J REED

ACTIONOPOLIS
Published by Komikwerks, LLC
1 Ruth Street Worcester, MA 01602

KOMIKWERKS

Created by Actionopolis, Gary Reed and Rick Hoberg
Based on a concept by Shannon Eric Denton and Patrick Coyle

First Edition

Printed in China.

DISTRIBUTED BY PUBLISHERS GROUP WEST

Library of Congress Cataloging-in-Publication Data
Reed, Gary
Spirit of the Samurai: Of Swords and Rings / Gary Reed and Rick Hoberg
p. cm. – (Spirit of the Samurai: Of Swords and Rings ; 1)
Summary: When a thirteen-year-old girl discovers the secret of her family's
ancestors, she is drawn into an ancient conflict still waged by the spirits of rival
samurai.
ISBN: 0-9778809-9-0
[1. Legends–Juvenile Fiction. 2. Brothers and Sisters–Juvenile Fiction.]
I. Hoberg, Rick II. Title
2006902386

Other books from

• The Anubis Tapestry •

• Blackfoot Braves Society •

• The Forest King •

• Heir to Fire •

• What I Did On My Hypergalactic
Interstellar Summer Vacation •

• Zombie Monkey Monster Jamboree •

And more coming soon!

For more information on
Spirit of the Samurai or any of our
other exciting books, visit our website:
www.actionopolis.com

TABLE OF CONTENTS

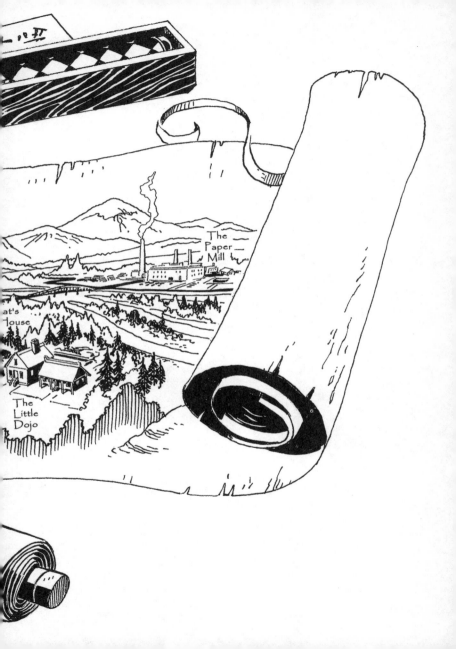

*To Albert Thayer, my "Uncle Al",
who may not have had the code of the
samurai, but gave me a moral compass
that I am honored to pass along
to my children.
—Gary*

*For my parents Dick and Alma Hoberg
who encouraged me, and for my
wife Aleta who sustains me.
—Rick*

SPIRIT OF THE SAMURAI

CHAPTER ONE
A Brother's Anger

Katherine Anderson saw that her brother, David, was really mad.

"Good," she whispered to herself. She smiled as he charged at her, screaming in frustration. She knew that when he was mad like this, he wasn't thinking too clearly and that gave her the advantage…again.

As David lunged to grab her, Katherine slipped her left foot between his feet, twisted her body out of the way, and let the momentum of David's weight carry him past her. He landed on the ground hard, and she heard a grunt as the air was knocked out of him.

Katherine laughed and wondered how many times

David would fall for that move. She tried to control herself because if she laughed too hard, he would get even madder.

She offered her hand to help David up, but he slapped it away. "Yep," she said. "You're mad." Katherine was getting used to it. He was always angry about something nowadays.

David glared at her as he stood, his dark eyes flashing angrily. At fourteen, he was a year older than Katherine, and she suddenly realized how much bigger he had gotten over the last year. They had been about the same size for as long as she could remember, but now he was growing fast and looking down at her.

Then David smiled. "You got me good that time, Kat." Katherine, or Kat, as she was usually called, sighed with relief. She didn't want David mad at her and for some reason, she had felt uneasy when he glared at her just moments ago.

Kat turned to leave. "C'mon, David, you know how upset Grandfather gets if we're late."

Grandfather was a man who lived by rules. And since he was raising Kat and David, they had to live by rules…his rules. But Kat didn't mind because Grandfather…and that's Grandfather, never Grandpa or Papa…was kind and fair. He had his rules, but they were simple. Be on time, be nice to others, don't be selfish, and respect everything. Of course, his main rule was to do as he said, but all adults said that.

Suddenly, Kat felt a hard force hit her back. It made her lose her breath and as she was falling, she realized that David's arms were wrapped around her. She saw the leaves on the ground, and knew that her face was about to hit them.

She landed with a thud and David landed on top of her. It hurt. She felt herself being turned around, but there was no time to react. Now, David sat on top of her and held her arms down. She felt his weight on her chest and she couldn't breathe. As she looked up, the sun was shining in her eyes, and David's face was just a shadow.

"You're not so quick now, are you?" said David as he sneered at Kat.

She struggled to get free, but couldn't move. She realized that David was stronger than her, much stronger. She wondered when that had happened, but she also knew that they were growing into teenagers, and that's when boys got strong and girls…well, girls didn't.

"I'm getting tired of you making a fool of me," David said between clenched teeth. "You always want to play these games and you think it's funny."

Kat looked into the shadow where David's face was supposed to be, the sunlight behind him blinding her.

"That's because I'm better than you," she said. She tried to say it as a joke, but they both knew it was true.

Now she could see David's face as he leaned towards her, and she was shocked at the look in his eyes. He was more than mad. He glared at her with hatred. "Better than me?" he yelled. "You aren't better than me now, are you?"

David leaned closer, his face next to hers. He stared at her with an expression she had never seen before. His weight seemed heavier, his arms pushed her into the ground–Kat felt trapped and everything was closing in on her. She felt helpless and wanted to cry, but she didn't want to give in to David.

"David! Get off!" Kat realized she was screaming. She twisted and turned, but nothing she did even budged him. She saw his face, the eyes glaring, his teeth clenched together. It made her afraid.

The tears came. She was usually embarrassed about crying, but if that's what it took to get David off, she didn't care. More than anything, she wanted him off her.

"David! Get off of her!" Kat turned at the voice. She was never so glad to see Grandfather.

Grandfather approached slowly. Kat wanted him to grab David and throw him off. But he didn't. He stood there and just looked at David.

"David. I said to get off of her." Grandfather's voice was stern, but Kat didn't feel David letting up at all, and he wouldn't look away from her.

"David." Grandfather took a step closer and his voice got louder.

Kat felt David start to relax, but before he rose, David squeezed her wrists hard and leaned back towards her face. "Next time, Grandfather won't be around. Then we'll see who's better once and for all."

David let go and stood. He didn't look at

Grandfather or Kat as he walked back to the house. Kat wiped the tears from her face as she got up. She couldn't stop shaking.

Grandfather watched David walk away, then looked back at Kat, but he didn't say anything. He waited until Kat stood next to him, and then started walking towards the house. Kat felt like she had done something wrong.

CHAPTER TWO
Another Lesson Learned

Kat walked a couple of steps behind Grandfather. She knew his silent moments, so she didn't say anything. They approached the house before Grandfather turned and asked her to join him in the garden.

In the garden, Kat sat down on the wooden bench in the center. Grandfather sat next to her. Neither of them said anything for a while.

Kat glanced at her Grandfather. Calling him that made him seem older than he was. Of course, he was old enough to be a grandfather, but he didn't seem that old to her.

At school, during parent conferences where Kat

volunteered to help out, she had a chance to meet her classmates' parents. Some of the parents were very young, yet others seemed older than Grandfather. It was at times like these meetings that Kat wished she had regular parents like most of the other kids. Even divorced parents were better than none. Grandfather never came to the conferences, but would schedule private meetings with the teachers instead.

Kat knew that Grandfather tried hard to give David and her a normal life. Their house was a lot like the other kids' houses. David and she kept up with the same things on TV and in music as their classmates. Kat and her brother were pretty much like other kids living in the suburbs of Seattle. However, when Kat asked about her and David's parents, Grandfather told her that they had died in an accident, but never anything more.

Kat knew there was something else going on. Something different. Even though they lived in the suburbs, their house was at the end of the street, and the backyard went into a wooded area that was fenced off. She had been surprised when she found out that her grandfather owned all that land and refused to sell it, no matter how much money he was offered. She was just getting old enough to start wondering how Grandfather could afford everything, since he didn't work.

Although they had a nice house, Grandfather spent much of his time in a smaller house in the woods, on the other side of the garden. Kat and David were only permitted to go there if they were with Grandfather. The small house, which Grandfather called the dojo, had no chairs, only floor mats. Next to the dojo was a large wooden room that Grandfather would exercise in every morning and where he would also bring Kat and David for training.

Grandfather didn't call it training. He called it teaching. Whatever it was called, Kat enjoyed it. David used to, but now he groaned whenever it was time for training. Grandfather always talked of everything as learning, and when he looked at her now on the garden bench, Kat knew she was about to get another lesson.

"So, Katherine, what did you learn?" Grandfather asked.

Kat didn't think too long. "That David's a mean brat."

Grandfather sighed.

Kat smiled. "Okay, I didn't learn that today. I already knew that."

Grandfather gave her his look that told Kat this was not a time for jokes.

Kat stared at her feet. "I learned that, even though I am better at training than David is, that doesn't matter if someone doesn't fight fair."

She glanced up to see if she was on the path to a right answer.

"You expect everyone to play by the rules?"

Kat smiled again. "Okay, I learned that, too."

Grandfather picked up two twigs from the ground. He held the twigs so that Kat could see them. "Look at these two sticks. One is thick and strong. The other seems to be thin and weak." Grandfather brushed his hand quickly over the two twigs and the larger one snapped. "The thick one has strength, but it cannot bend, while the thin one will bend when a strong force hits it. So, although only one appears to have strength, actually both of them do. They just have different ways of being strong."

Kat scrunched up her face. "So, both me and David are strong, but in different ways?"

Grandfather dropped the sticks. "Yes, but I suspect you already knew that. What else did you learn?"

Kat looked down again, thinking. Then she thought back on David being on top of her and how she couldn't get him off. "I learned that David and I were once the same as far as strength. But now he is much stronger."

Grandfather smiled. "Yes. Before, you were both the same stick. Now, he has become the thick stick and you are the stick that bends. Why is that?"

Kat knew the answer. She was a good student and

she paid attention in all of her classes, including the health education ones. "Because he's a boy and I'm a girl. Because he is growing into a man, and a man has much more strength than a woman."

Grandfather stood. "Yes. You two are at an age where things are changing. He is no longer your equal. He will grow taller, bigger, and stronger."

Kat nodded. "So, he will always be better

than me now?"

Kat's grandfather patted her on the head as he started to leave. "I didn't say that. Yes, David will be stronger, but that's not necessarily better. It's just different. After all, it is water that wears down the rock, even though the rock is much harder."

CHAPTER THREE
Into the Darkness

The next day, Kat rode the school bus home in silence. There weren't many students on her route and following some rule that she thought was stupid, Kat had to sit with all the other seventh graders, in the middle of the bus. The front was for sixth graders and the back was for eighth grade students.

She saw David in the back, but he didn't want her talking to him on the bus or in school. It was not cool for a guy to have a kid sister hanging around. That didn't really bother Kat too much, since she and David had never been close. To her, they just happened to live in the same house. Kat was sure that David felt the same way, but recently he had become even more distant. Their house was far from all the other houses, so the two of them were always the last on the bus, and they always sat in silence.

Grandfather was in the garden as usual when she got home. David went straight into the house, probably to watch MTV's newest game show. Kat always liked to tell Grandfather what she did in school that day, and he seemed to enjoy listening to her. David used to do the same, but he rarely spoke to Grandfather any more, and since he didn't talk with her, Kat felt that David must be pretty lonely.

Kat told Grandfather the day's events, and he smiled and laughed at all the right places in her stories. After she finished, he looked at his watch.

"It's time for another hunt, Kat. I'll head to the dojo in one hour. See if you can hide from me." He tapped her nose and left.

It was a game that Kat and her grandfather played often. She would hide somewhere along the path between the garden and the dojo, and he had to find her as he walked along the path. Grandfather almost always found her, but David rarely did, so he had quit playing a long time ago. In fact, it seemed that David had little to do with her or Grandfather nowadays.

Kat wondered how Grandfather always found her, and thought maybe he spied on her and watched where she hid, just so he could find her and make her work harder. As Grandfather always said, he was just teaching her.

So, instead of waiting until the hour was up, Kat decided not to wait until the last moment to hide like she normally did. That way there was no chance Grandfather could see where she hid. She ran down the path and started looking where she could hide.

The trees were losing their leaves, and Kat thought about the tricks Grandfather had taught her over the years. She scooped up fallen leaves and made a large pile around a small tree. Then Kat lay down and wrapped herself around the trunk, so when she pulled the leaves over herself the shape of the pile wouldn't look like a body. To someone walking by, it would look like the leaves got caught by the wind and wrapped around the tree. Kat smiled to herself. Like Grandfather always said, the best place to hide was in plain sight.

Kat lay in the leaves and remembered her Grandfather's lessons. Lie still, slow down your breathing, and think about something to take your mind off the waiting. She had learned this lesson well, and could lie in a

spot for hours without moving.

She thought about the training that she and David had to do every day. They had been training for as long as Kat could remember. She liked it, but she would never tell anyone about it, not even her friends at school. She looked at it as exercise, like her friends' gymnastics or soccer, but other kids might find it strange to see a brother and sister in suburban Seattle training with swords, knives, and throwing weapons. Kat was always eager to practice more, but David always left once the sword training ended. Grandfather stayed with Kat, showing her moves that she called judo but he said was something else, an ancient style that didn't even have a name. Kat asked him once about why he knew such things and why he was teaching them, and he said he would tell her and David when they were old enough and not before.

Kat felt herself growing tired under the leaves and her eyes started to close. Then she heard a noise. She could see though a small hole in the pile and waited for

Grandfather's feet to walk by. She smiled. He was early; it hadn't been an hour yet.

A shadow approached, and Kat knew it didn't belong to Grandfather. It was David. She wondered what he was doing. They were never supposed to go to the dojo unless Grandfather was with them. That was one of his rules.

Kat waited until David passed and then she slowly stood, letting the leaves fall off. She followed David, staying far enough behind so he couldn't hear her. She wasn't worried about David seeing her, as he wasn't looking back. Even if he did, she was good at hiding. She used to follow David all the time and he had never spotted her.

She saw David enter the dojo and she crept to the door. David headed right towards the back, where the training area was. That was forbidden! Kat wasn't sure what to do. Should she follow David? Or should she run and tell Grandfather? She didn't know what to do!

Kat thought for a minute, then made her decision. She entered the darkness of the dojo.

CHAPTER FOUR
Secrets Revealed

I t was very dark inside. The room had no electricity, and the walls were solid with no windows, but the roof was raised a few inches above the walls, and that allowed a little bit of light to come in. Kat saw the cloudy sky through this gap and through a large overhang in the roof that kept out the rain…most of the time.

Kat and David always called the dojo, "the barn," since it was large and had a dirt floor covered with straw mats. There were only two doors, one that came from the dojo house and another door that led to Grandfather's temple. She and David were not allowed in the temple. She had never even seen the inside of it.

Now the temple door was open and David was inside. Grandfather was sure to come soon and she knew that he would be mad at David…and mad at her if she went in.

She walked along the wall until she reached the temple door. Holding her breath, she peeked inside. It was dark except for some lit candles. At the far end was an altar. On the walls to either side hung large paintings. Kat couldn't make them out at first, but as her eyes adjusted to the dark she saw that they were of samurai warriors in battle.

Kat snuck in, keeping an eye on David, who was lighting more candles at the altar. The wall behind her was adorned with many different kinds of weapons. On each side of the door were three sets of samurai armor. Kat barely had time to wonder why Grandfather had all of this before David spoke.

"It's time you saw this," David said without turning. "He has kept it from us for too long."

Kat stepped forward, a little uneasy, as she wasn't sure why David wasn't mad. She asked, "Kept what from us?"

David waved his arm around the room. "This…all of this. It belongs to us, not to Grandfather." David moved toward the altar as he turned to look at her. "It's ours. Can't you see that?"

"No." Kat wanted to leave before Grandfather came.

David lifted a book that was lying on the altar. "It's all in here. Grandfather never told us, so I found out for myself."

Kat inched closer, now more curious than scared. "I don't know what you're talking about."

"We're special." David sat down on the altar with the

book in his lap. "It's all in here."

David told Kat about what was in the book. It was a history of the great warriors of Japan called the samurai. Trained from youth, samurai were taught to fight with great swords called katanas, made by only the finest sword-smiths in the country. The samurai served their masters, the Shogun, and swore allegiance to their master for life.

He told her about the great battles between two major clans of Japan–the Toho Clan and the Clan of the Black Rings–hundreds of years ago. Both clans had samurai warriors, but the Clan of the Black Rings were said to be samurai warriors that had died and were brought back to life. They no longer served their Shogun, but the leader of the Black Rings, Lord Hiro. The four rings of Hiro were forged from a meteor that had crashed into his village. Hiro was trying to take over the other clans and kill all the samurai so that the risen warriors would serve only him.

The samurai of the Toho Clan, led by Lord Toho, were the only ones who could stand against the dark warriors of Hiro. Toho had the greatest sword-smith in the land, Niatato, make special swords that could slay the undead samurai. These katanas were made of a special metal called Heavensblade. Heavensblade was metal made of steel and gold flecks that fell from a comet. For years, Toho and his samurai warriors fought against Hiro's Clan of the Black Rings, but neither side could gain the advantage.

As the years passed, the brave samurai of Toho fell, as did the Clan of the Black Rings, until only Toho and Hiro were left. They stood on the Plain of Mimsota, each knowing it would be the end of one of them in this final battle. If Toho fell, he knew that Hiro would bring him back from the dead to serve the evil Lord, and then Hiro would rebuild his undead army.

David stepped down from the altar and pointed to one large painting. "That shows the great battle between

Toho and Hiro. All the Heavensblade swords were destroyed except for Toho's. His sword was special because his blood was mixed in when they were forging the sword."

Kat looked at the painting of two warriors with their great swords locked in combat. She guessed which one was Lord Hiro of The Clan of the Black Rings. His sword had four rings built into the handle, one for each of Hiro's fingers. His armor was black, and on the chest plate was an emblem of four interlocking rings. Toho wore armor of red and gold, and his katana, made of the Heavensblade metal, shone more like gold than silver.

Kat was thrilled by the story. She asked David excitedly, "What happened?"

David stared at the painting. He didn't have to look at the book to finish the story. "At the time of this battle, Hiro and Toho were old, and had lost most of their strength. Still, they fought for hours, each of them suffering severe wounds. Even the winner would probably not live to see another day."

David explained that finally the two warriors just stood there, the life draining out of them. They had fought into the night, but neither could raise their sword to finish the battle. Both of them were dying. As they stood there, each breathing their last breath, they caught sight of a rare and stunning event, The Dragon's Tail, a brilliant comet blazing across the sky.

David turned from the picture. "Both of their swords began to glow, and they realized that their magic–the rings of Hiro and the Heavensblade metal of Toho's katana–were made of the same metal. The metal that fell from The Dragon's Tail comet."

David clapped his hands. "Then the two swords were yanked from their hands and came together. People watching the battle said the two swords crossed and hung in mid-air, glowing first silver, then red, then gold, until with a flash, the swords fell to the ground. At the same time, Toho and Hiro dropped to the ground, both dead."

David walked up to Kat. "That is what Grandfather

has been keeping from us."

Kat looked with surprise at David. "It's just a story, David."

"Just a story! Don't you get it?" David's eyes flashed with anger as he pointed at the painting. "Toho! His sword belongs to us. He was our ancestor!"

Kat was shocked. "We're Japanese?"

"Yes."

Both Kat and David turned when they heard Grandfather's voice as he entered the dojo. He told them, "You both have the blood of the greatest of the Japanese warriors in you."

Kat looked at David, then at Grandfather. "But we don't look Japanese…and you don't either."

"It's a long story and for another day." Grandfather approached the two of them. His face was stern. "The question should be, what are you two doing in here?"

"No," said David as he walked towards the altar. "It's our turn for questions."

Kat was stunned. David was sounding much older than his fourteen years and he spoke to Grandfather with a lack of respect. Kat didn't like it.

"I know everything, Grandfather," David said as he held up the book. "I read the chronicles."

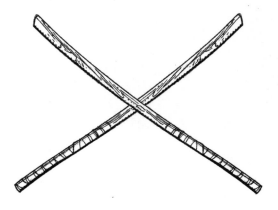

Grandfather smiled. "As Kat said, David, they're just stories."

"No, they're not!" screamed David. "And I found more." David stepped towards Grandfather and held up a small empty box. "I found the rings."

Grandfather looked surprised. "What did you do

with them, David? Where are they?"

David held up his right hand. He was wearing three rings. "That's the secret, isn't it, Grandfather? The swords and the rings–they must be together."

Kat stood next to her Grandfather. She didn't like David's attitude, but Grandfather seemed more concerned about the rings then David's lack of respect.

David glared at Grandfather. "When were you going to tell us? Were you even going to tell us?"

Grandfather held his hand towards David. "There is so much you don't know. It's dangerous. Please, give me the rings and I'll explain everything. I promise."

David walked towards his sister. He seemed calmer now. "Haven't you ever wondered, Kat, why we go through all of this training? It's not just exercise. It's to prepare us."

"Prepare us for what?" Kat moved closer to her Grandfather and looked at him. "What's David talking about?"

David jumped to the altar. Hanging above the altar were two crossed wooden swords. He went to grab one.

Kat felt Grandfather move away from her and towards David. She was shocked at how fast he moved.

"No, don't touch them!" Grandfather yelled as he rushed towards David.

David's hand stopped, but he didn't move away. "Why not, Grandfather? They're just wooden swords, like the ones we practice with."

David held out his hand with the rings on it. "Don't come any closer."

Grandfather stopped.

David looked at Kat. "See, Kat, they look like wooden swords, but once I touch one, the sword's magic will be restored. These are the swords of Toho and Hiro."

"But this will only work if a blood relative touches it, and it has to be tonight, because that is when The Dragon's Tail returns."

Grandfather was shocked. "How did you know that?"

Kat looked at Grandfather. "You mean the stories are true?"

"Oh they're true, aren't they, Grandfather?" David's voice sounded more like an accusation than a question.

"Yes, David, it's true that the comet will bring them back, but you don't understand everything. Please, don't–" Grandfather pleaded.

"Too late." David put his hand over one of the crossed wooden swords. "I know that as soon as I grab the Heavensblade, I will have the power of Toho. It's why you trained me in sword fighting, so that I could use the power."

As David placed his hand on the wooden hilt, he looked at Kat. "It's in our blood. The power belongs to us."

David grabbed the wooden sword and raised it in the

air, waiting for the power to be unleashed.

Nothing happened.

Kat was relieved. And then she giggled. It was a nervous giggle, but she was so happy that all of this had just been nonsense, just stories.

But when she looked at Grandfather, she could tell he was even more scared.

David stood there, looking confused as he stared at the wooden sword. "I don't understand," he said quietly.

David let the wooden sword drop from his hand as he looked at Grandfather. "It's the night of the Dragon's Tail."

Grandfather spoke softly. "David, please, come here. I'll explain everything."

Then David looked at the second sword on the wall and reached for it.

Grandfather rushed towards David again. "No!"

It was too late. As soon as David's hand touched the sword, Kat saw the weapon change from wood to gleaming black metal. The sword glowed and electric bolts shot from it.

The bolts bounced around the room. Kat saw one hit Grandfather, and he crumpled to the floor. Then she saw a flash of light and something p u s h e d against her, like someone hitting her, and she felt dizzy. Kat dropped to her knees and felt herself losing consciousness.

As her eyes started to close, there was another flash of lightning and she saw David holding the wooden sword. Then she saw a samurai warrior in black armor holding a black katana. Then it went back to David with the wooden sword. With every flash it kept going back and forth.

The last thing Kat saw before she passed out was the handle of the black sword. It had three rings on it and inside the rings were David's fingers.

CHAPTER FIVE
A Stranger She Knew

K at opened her eyes. She saw the night sky. It was very dark, with the moon hidden by clouds. Then she remembered what just happened.

She sat up quickly and saw that she was on a bench in the garden. Her grandfather sat on the bench opposite her, wrapping his ankle with a piece of cloth.

"What happened?" Kat stood, then quickly sat back down because she felt dizzy.

Grandfather answered without looking at her. "I twisted my ankle carrying you out here."

Kat stood up again, leaning on the bench. "David! What happened to David?" She took a few steps towards the dojo, but Grandfather's voice stopped her

"Wait, Kat. I must explain some things first."

Kat looked at her Grandfather as she came back to the bench. For the first time, he looked old. "So, it's true? All of it is true?" she asked.

Grandfather nodded his head. "Yes, it's all true, but it's more than what David told you. There's more, much more."

Kat sat next to her grandfather, who stared at the ground as he started to talk.

"After the great battle at Mimosa, the two swords were almost welded together, bound together by the shared metal of the comet. They stayed that way until a solar eclipse three days later. The blood of the great warriors that had dried on the swords began to boil, and the swords steamed as if they were on fire. The next day, the swords turned to wood and separated, or so it appeared to everyone who didn't have the power to see them for what they really were. If you were of Toho's bloodline or Hiro's bloodline, you could see the swords as the katanas of the great warriors if you just touched them. But the swords could not be restored unless they were touched during the appearance of the comet, The Dragon's Tail."

Grandfather explained that each sword was returned to its family. The custom was to bury a katana with its warrior, but since the swords had turned to wood, it didn't seem fitting to do that. After eighteen years, the Dragon's Tail comet returned, and Hiro's son restored his katana. The grandson of Toho did the same, and again there was a great battle. Toho's grandson won the battle and kept both of the swords. When Toho's grandson died, the katanas became wood again.

The family of Toho realized that they had to protect their family and their country from Hiro's relatives obtaining the sword again. Each generation was trained in the samurai way so any attempt at stealing Hiro's sword by the members of Hiro's family or the Clan of the Black Rings could be stopped.

Kat thought for a moment. "Why didn't they just destroy the sword?"

"The swords hold the energy of the clans inside of them. They are not wood, even though that is all that we may see. The Heavensblade and the rings, they were forged by the comet. They cannot be destroyed until the last member of the clan is gone.

"That is the legacy of both families," Grandfather continued, "and it has been that way for hundreds of years."

"So, that's why you trained us?" Kat asked. "So we could protect the swords?"

"Yes," Grandfather said, "but it was David who was to be trained in the samurai ways. You were trained in the arts of the ninjitsu-the shadow warriors."

"Ninjitsu?"

Grandfather finally looked up at Kat. "Ninjitsu. The ninja. Samurai training is reserved for the eldest son. Brothers and sisters of the eldest son were trained in the ninja way so that they too could serve."

Grandfather stared at the night sky. "But you were different, Kat. At first, I trained you to be David's partner, but you took to the training well. Much better than David.

So, you learned both ways."

Kat watched her grandfather as she thought about what she had just seen. "Why didn't David restore the Heavensblade when he touched it?" she asked.

"Because he was wearing the rings." Kat and her Grandfather both turned to look at the figure of a man coming from the shadows.

Kat was gripped by fear, but Grandfather looked into the darkness as the man approached.

"Or," the man said as he came closer, "should I say, he was wearing three of the rings."

Grandfather stood, a little shaky, unable to put weight on his twisted ankle. "Kyoshi?"

The man came closer and Grandfather reached his hand out to touch the man's face. "Kyoshi, is it really you?" Grandfather had to sit back down, as he seemed to get weak. Kat stepped away. She didn't know who this man was, but she didn't want to get too close.

Kat watched and was surprised as the man knelt before Grandfather and laid his head on the older man's lap. "Yes, it's me."

Kat stared as Grandfather bent over to hug the man. For the first time ever, she saw her grandfather cry. She was confused. Who was this man? How did he know what happened?

Grandfather lifted the man's head and whispered to him. Kat felt uncomfortable and didn't know what was going on. She felt even more uncomfortable when Grandfather pointed towards her and the man turned to look at her.

When the man got up and started coming toward her, Kat didn't know whether to run or not. So, she sat down. It helped her from trembling. She looked at Grandfather and he was smiling. His eyes were full of tears, yet he was smiling.

The man stopped in front of her. "This is Katherine?"

Grandfather nodded. "We call her Kat."

The man knelt in front of her. "Hi Kather-er, Kat."

Kat gave a quick smile and a quick wave. She felt stupid, but she didn't know what else to do. When he said his next words, Kat found herself getting weak again and almost passed out.

The man looked into her eyes and said, "I'm your father."

CHAPTER SIX
To Serve the Black Rings

I f someone were to look at the dojo at the end of the path from the garden, they would see a teenage boy standing still and clutching a wooden sword. The boy stared straight ahead with his feet firmly planted, and didn't seem to notice the wind that picked up leaves and swirled them in front of his face.

However, if they had the power that David had, then they would see what David saw. He did not see boy's hands holding a sword of wood, but rather an ebony blazoned katana that he held with gloves made of laced steel. He was not wearing ordinary clothes, but instead glistening black armor with four rings decorating the breastplate.

Instead of the dusty twilight sky with raindrops beginning to appear, David saw a hazy mist covering the land. In this world he had entered, there was no night, no day, but always a cloudy gray.

This world, this shadow realm that allowed him to hold the powerful katana of Hiro, Lord of The Black Rings, was not complete. The only way to restore it fully was to bring the fourth ring back to the sword that he clutched in his hand. But even with just the three rings, he would have enough power to defeat anyone who would dare to pick up the Heavensblade.

David took a deep breath. He felt good. He knew that this was his place, this was his right destiny. He had the bloodline running through him and he could hear the faded voices of those who wanted to join him. David wanted them to join, too. He wanted the spirits of all the samurai who had died throughout history serving the Clan of the Black Rings. He clutched the sword closer to his chest. He would restore them.

David waited. He waited to see who would come to

him for the sword of Toho. He knew that whoever it was, they would have to be struck down, and Toho's awakened katana pried from their dead fingers. No one could stop David from getting the Heavensblade sword, and after that, the fourth ring. Then, the shadow world would become real again. It would have the sun, the moon, the day and the night. And it would have the rebirth of the Clan of the Black Rings.

David knew all of this because he heard the whispers in his ear, the whispers of the great Hiro who spoke to him across the ages.

CHAPTER SEVEN
The Past Unveiled

Kat looked into the eyes of the man who said he was her father.

His eyes were almost black. His hair was darker than hers. He looked part Japanese, but not completely. She saw his hand trembling as he reached to gently touch her face.

"My father is dead," Kat said as she backed away.

Kyoshi stood up. Kat could tell he was sad but not surprised at what she said. She didn't mean to sound harsh, but for as long as she could remember she was told her father was dead. How could he not be dead? Everything was moving too fast and everything was wrong.

Kat got up and ran to her Grandfather. She hoped that he could make everything like it was before, but one look at his face told her that it would never go back. Grandfather hugged her and she heard him whisper, "I'm so sorry it all happened this way, Kat...so sorry." It was then that Kat felt warm tears start to roll down her face.

Grandfather stood, still hugging her. "We'll go back to the house. There is much to talk about."

Kat pulled away and started back towards the dojo. "What about David? We can't just leave him back there!"

Kyoshi grabbed her. His grip was strong, like a steel vise, but she could tell that he was not trying to hurt her. "No, Kat." He said it simply, but it was enough to tell her that it was no use arguing the point. She pulled away from him and ran to her grandfather, who was already hobbling up the trail towards the house.

Inside, Kat sat at the kitchen table with Kyoshi.

Neither of them spoke. Grandfather made tea and as Kat watched him, she began to realize how many aspects of their lives were from Japanese culture. The tea was not from tea bags, but green tea leaves in a bag with Japanese characters. She thought about the food they prepared, such as beef and rice or chicken and soba, or buckwheat noodles, and how they used chopsticks. The snacks they ate: sanbei and rice crackers instead of chips; mochi, sticky rice cakes wrapped in seaweed strips they called nori instead of microwave pizza; and pocky sticks instead of candy bars. That didn't make them Japanese, though, did it?

Grandfather poured tea for the three of them. "I know you're worried about David, Kat. We all are. But some things must be explained so you understand what it is we must do now. David is not the same David any more. He is Hiro now. You may see him holding a wooden sword, but that's only what it seems to be."

Her grandfather sat down. "He has great power now,

but doesn't know how to use it completely. But he will learn and there will be many to teach him. Then he will become their master, and even those that die will continue to serve him and the Clan of the Black Ring."

"And the sword can't be destroyed?" Kat blurted out.

"No, Kat, the sword and David are now one," Grandfather said. "Even if we could take it away, it would not take away his power. It would weaken him, but it would not bring David back."

Kat thought there must be some answer. "So, we just need to get the other sword?"

"It's not that simple. The Sword of Toho must be held by someone with the bloodline in them." Grandfather nodded towards Kyoshi. "I do not have the bloodline, so it must be your father."

Kat glanced at Kyoshi before turning back to her grandfather, who looked away as Kyoshi spoke. "I have the blood, and though I do not deserve the honor of Toho, I will take the sword and do what must be done. There is no choice."

Kat looked at Grandfather, who stared at his tea. She refused to look at Kyoshi, but she could tell that he was staring at her. Kat sipped her tea and it burned her lips, but it gave her something to do while everyone sat quietly. She took another sip and burned her lips again.

Kat cupped her tea and felt the heat in her hands. "What do you mean, Grandfather, when you say that you do not have the bloodline?"

Grandfather looked at her and started to speak. "I was born in Japan, but my parents were Americans who had come over before the war and ran an English speaking school. When World War Two broke out, they had to stay, as the government of Japan wouldn't let them leave. They stayed outside of Tokyo for the entire war.

"I was three years old when the war finally ended. The United States started to rebuild Japan, and my parents were only too happy to be a part of that, so we stayed. I grew up in Japan, and for all intents and purposes I was Japanese. I didn't look like it, but it was my culture."

Grandfather smiled. Kat felt good that he smiled. "Then when I was at the University, I met the woman who would become your grandmother. Her name was Myota, and she was the most beautiful person I had ever seen. At first, she didn't want anything to do with me, but I finally wore her down. It took me over two years, but I finally got her to marry me."

"Your father," Grandfather said, pointing at Kyoshi, "was our first born. I had no idea of everything that would happen when he was born. It was then that your grandmother's father explained the history of their family to me. Your grandmother was of the Toho clan, and we had to teach young Kyoshi all the lessons that you've been learning."

Grandfather looked down. "I was honored to carry out such a duty. Even though I was called a gaijin—an outsider—by some because I wasn't Japanese, most of your grandmother's family accepted me because I chose to be Japanese instead of being born into it. And when your grandmother was killed in a car accident, her family continued to treat me as one of their own."

Kat watched as her grandfather stopped talking. She knew he was remembering Myota.

Kyoshi realized this as well, and started talking. "Your grandfather trained me and also my brother, Onwa. Neither of us thought much of it, though. It seemed to be tales of old legends. Although your grandfather loved the Japanese culture, I was more interested in my American side. I desperately wanted to go to the United States, so it was agreed that I would attend college here. Everyone in Japan knew how important it was to understand the American way. I could speak English and attended schools to learn Western customs, so it wasn't hard to fit right in when I got here.

"It was at school that I met your mother. As you know, her name was Amy. She was a typical California girl with her blonde hair and blue eyes."

Grandfather tapped Kat's hand as he smiled at her. "Now you see why you don't look Japanese. But you do have the blood running through you."

Kyoshi stood as he started talking again. Kat could tell it was getting harder for him to talk about her mother. "What I didn't know was that your mother was from the Hiro clan. It had been decided many generations ago that the Hiro clan would move to different countries to spread out across the world. Your mother was born and raised in America. No one could tell she had Japanese blood, but she was taught many of the ancient customs. She was of two worlds.

"It was arranged for your mother to meet me so that she could find out why a member of the Toho clan was in the United States. She didn't want to do it, but her family had asked. To her, it was almost a game and she was just humoring her relatives. She told me later that in her mind, I was to be a one night date and no more. But she saw that I wanted nothing to do with the legends of Toho and cared little about the swords and the duties that were expected of me. She felt the same way, and I think that was a bond that grew between us. We both looked to the future, not the past."

Kyoshi swallowed hard before he spoke again, but

his voice was weaker. "The legends of the swords and the legacy of the Toho clan meant nothing to us. We had no idea that it was not up to us. We couldn't forget about the past, the ancient past. Our families wouldn't let us."

He turned and looked at Kat. "It killed your mother. It killed your mother all because of this duty that we inherited by birth. A duty that neither one of us wanted."

Grandfather put his arm on Kyoshi's shoulder.

Kyoshi bowed his head and Kat could see that he was fighting back tears.

"Kat," Grandfather said, "it is time for you to get some sleep. I need to talk to your father alone."

Kat protested. "What about David? We can't just leave him!"

Grandfather held his hand up. "Kat. There is nothing we can do tonight. Tomorrow will be a new day and we will have new answers."

Kat hesitated. How could they think of sending her

to bed now? David was still at the dojo. Her father who she had just met was sitting in front of her and telling her how her mother died. An ancient legend was coming true and she was finding out that she was all part of it. How could she go to bed? She couldn't leave now!

"But–"

Grandfather raised his hand. That was his way of telling her the discussion was over.

Kat protested. "It's not fair. I–"

Grandfather: "Kat! Now!"

She rarely saw such a stern look on her grandfather's face. Kat knew he was not going to change his mind. She got up and left.

CHAPTER EIGHT
Joining the Shadows

Kat walked into her room and turned on the television. She made sure it was loud. Not loud enough for Grandfather to tell her to turn it down, but loud enough to let him know that she was upset. Kat stepped outside of her room, slammed the door, and stood in the hallway.

It worked. Grandfather and Kyoshi had been quiet, but now they started talking again. Kat removed her shoes and silently made her way down the hallway as her grandfather had taught her. She slid along the carpet instead of stepping, so the floorboards wouldn't creak. She tilted the lampshade in the hallway to make sure that when she was by the kitchen doorway, no light was behind her to cast a shadow. Kat had to concentrate, but she could make out the men's voices.

Kat heard Grandfather ask Kyoshi, "How did you find us?"

Kyoshi's voice was still weak. "Remember when Amy and I tried to destroy the swords? When we thought we could end all of this hatred that has existed for centuries?"

"I remember," said Grandfather. "I also remember telling you that the swords are not of this realm. They cannot be destroyed. The sword only holds the power, it is not the power."

"We had to try, Father," Kyoshi said. "And yes, you were right."

"But what does that have to do with how you found us?"

"I found you because of this."

Kyoshi was showing Grandfather something, and Kat had to see it. She lay on the floor and stuck her head slightly into the doorway, knowing that it was less likely that she would be spotted at floor level. Kat saw Kyoshi holding a black ring.

Grandfather reacted with shock. "That's where the fourth ring was! You had it!"

"Before Amy died, she managed to remove one of the four rings from the sword of Hiro. It is all I have left of her."

Grandfather suddenly looked towards the hallway, sensing something. He slowly got up as Kyoshi continued, "I carried the ring with me always, and a few weeks ago it started to heat up, even burned me. It was then that I knew someone was wearing the other rings. I did some searching. I got a good idea of where you might be, and the ring was like a homing signal. I never realized that it would be David wearing the rings."

Kat's grandfather quickly peeked around the corner and looked into the hallway. He saw nothing there, so he went to Kat's room and carefully opened her door. She was on her bed with the television on, and yet was wearing her headphones to her stereo. He smiled and then sighed as he glanced at the door that led to David's room.

Kat waited for a minute after her grandfather had looked in on her. She had pretended not to notice him, but she had seen his reflection in her mirror. Kat knew he was just being protective, and didn't want her to get involved, but she was already involved. It was her brother that had been taken from her.

She pulled a bag out from under her bed. It contained the training gear that Grandfather had put together for her. Kat was supposed to only use it with him, but she had practiced with the equipment on her own. She grabbed a black bodysuit and put it on. She took a quick look at herself in the mirror before she tugged a mask down over her head and slipped out her window.

Kat ran down the path towards the dojo. She was glad it was raining hard. The mud softened the stones under her padded feet. The rain soaked through her bodysuit, but she knew that was for the best. A rain repellent on her clothes would make her outfit reflect moonlight, and that would not be helpful.

She stopped near the dojo. A figure stood in the rain outside the doorway, with the wooden sword cradled in his arms. David. It looked as if he was standing guard, and Kat realized that was exactly what he was doing.

A sheet of lightning flashed across the sky. As the silver light illuminated David, she saw a different figure instead of her brother. It was of a samurai warrior, dressed in black, and instead of a wooden sword he held the katana of Hiro. Kat gasped and then slapped her hand over her mouth, hoping that she had not been heard.

Kat cautiously backed deeper into the woods. She made sure not to put her full weight down on the ground, as Grandfather had taught her. Kat shifted her direction sideways, but always kept going backwards at the same time, so there wasn't a constant motion in one direction. Grandfather had taught her that the eye first sees motion, so when moving you had to keep breaking up the expected path.

Kat continued her slow progress to the back of the dojo. She resisted running, even though she wanted to. The key, Grandfather had always said, was time: "Take your time. Patience is your partner. Use it."

Kat found herself being thankful for the rain again as she put on her shuko, or cat's claws–sharp bones fashioned like claws that strapped to her palms. A larger version, known as ashiko, went on her feet. The bones had been stained black and sanded to eliminate gloss, and Grandfather had told her that bone was quieter than metal. She looked at the dojo's rear wall. It was roughly a ten-foot climb to the gap, and Kat figured the opening between the wall and the roof of the dojo was about a foot wide.

She took a few deep breaths. Although she didn't understand everything that was going on, she knew that it was important to get the sword of Toho. This was not a time for sitting in the kitchen drinking tea.

Kat spread her body out and dug the claws into the wall of the dojo. The rain splattered loudly enough that she could use more force to dig the claws in deeper. Again, she knew that she had to be patient. To take her time. It was also important to spread her body out as wide as possible to balance her weight.

She climbed slowly, letting her weight fall mainly on

her feet and using her hand claws to reach further with each grab. Kat felt herself sweating, and was glad the mask had rings around the eyeholes so her perspiration didn't get into her eyes. She pretended this was just another practice exercise. Kat didn't think about the ten-foot wall, but focused on climbing a few inches at a time.

At the top of the wall, she rolled through the small opening. It was at this point that Kat realized her mistake. She should have brought a rope! That would have made things so much easier. Now she would have to climb down and then climb back up. Kat gritted her teeth and silently called herself stupid before starting down the wall.

The climb down was harder. Kat was tempted to jump, but knew she couldn't until she was closer to the ground. The dojo was dark, so she couldn't be sure what was beneath her. Finally, after what seemed like hours, she stepped on a straw mat.

Kat crouched down and felt the ground, trying to remember where the wooden sword had fallen when David dropped it. As she crawled on the ground, she looked at the doorway and saw David standing there, still facing away from the dojo.

She moved silently, spreading her right hand out and sweeping it in front of her. Then she felt something move and realized she had bumped a candle. Kat tried to catch the candle before it rolled away, but she missed. The candle had a metal holder, and when it hit another candle, she heard the two bases clink. She lay flat and looked towards the door.

David heard the noise. He turned and slowly walked into the dojo, trying to peer into the darkness. Kat saw lightning flash in the distance, near enough to transform the silhouetted form standing in the doorway from David to the samurai warrior.

Kat slid back to the corner of the dojo. She knew she had to hide, so she bent herself to fit into the corner. Grandfather had taught her that the corner was the darkest spot in a room, and that she wouldn't look like a person by being bent like that. David, or what used to be David, looked around. He looked up at the opening, and Kat was so glad that she hadn't used a rope after all. He would have seen it.

David seemed satisfied, and stepped backward toward the doorway before turning again to watch anything

approaching the dojo. Kat stayed in the corner and didn't move until another lightning flash lit up the sky. This time she wasn't looking at the figure in the doorway but at the floor. And she saw it. Just for a moment, but she saw it. The sword.

Kat crawled to it and was about to pick it up when she remembered what had happened with David when he touched the sword. She didn't want that to happen. Kat looked around and saw the cloth that covered the table with the burned-out candles. She removed the candles and gently placed them on the ground.

The cloth was long and narrow, and Kat held one end in her hand as she grabbed the sword, wrapping the cloth around it. She tied the ends of the tablecloth together to make a sling-like carrier and slung the sword across her back.

She took one more glance at David and then climbed the wall to escape the dojo. She had the sword. Now, what was she going to do with it?

CHAPTER NINE
A Fateful Decision

Kat stepped into the kitchen, pleased with herself when she saw the shock on the two men's faces. She said nothing for a moment, letting the rain drip off her clothes. Then, she untied the makeshift sling and put the covered sword on the table.

"Now we can help David," she said as she removed her mask.

Kyoshi stammered as he stared at Kat. "H-how?"

Grandfather held back his smile. "I trained her well." Then he remembered the seriousness of the situation and sternly looked at Kat. "Did David see you?"

Kat shook her head. "No. But I saw him. He has the black armor, like in the painting."

Grandfather looked at Kyoshi. "Hiro."

Kyoshi just nodded and pointed to the sword. "Kat, when you touched the sword, did anything happen?"

Kat again shook her head. She realized she was shaking from the cold. "I never touched it. I wrapped it up, but I never touched it with my hands."

"Good, good," Kyoshi said as he pushed the sword towards his father. "You must unwrap it. If I touch it, then it will live through me. I am not ready yet to take on that responsibility."

As Grandfather took the tablecloth off the sword, Kat leaned on the table to see the sword. It was simple wood, much like the swords they practiced with. "How do you know this is Toho's sword, Grandfather?" she asked. "After all, nothing happened when David touched it."

Grandfather held the sword in his hands. "David had the blood of Toho and Hiro in him. Perhaps it was the rings, but he is more Hiro than Toho. He could only be one, not both."

Kyoshi stepped towards the table. "It is the Heavensblade. I can feel it. It calls for me to take it. Only one that has Toho blood would feel such a calling."

Kat understood what he was saying. She heard the call as well. When she held the blade, she heard voices whispering to her and although very faint, she heard what sounded like swords clanging and the thundering of horses running.

Kyoshi bowed his head. "I need time before I take it. I—" Kyoshi stopped and turned away.

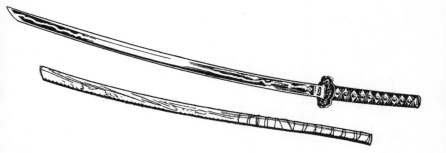

Kat looked at Grandfather as he took her hand. "Kat, it's too late for David," he said. "Once the Clan of the Black Rings has taken someone, they are forever under the power."

Grandfather faced her. She could see his eyes were watery. "David," he said, "cannot be helped now. He can only be stopped."

Kat pulled away. She had an idea of what Grandfather was saying, but she couldn't believe it. She didn't want to believe it.

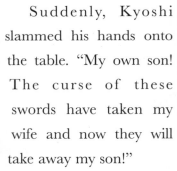

Suddenly, Kyoshi slammed his hands onto the table. "My own son! The curse of these swords have taken my wife and now they will take away my son!"

Kat backed away. It all was clear now. They had to stop David. They were planning to kill him. "No, you can't do it!" she screamed.

Kyoshi closed his eyes for a moment. She could see the pain he felt, but his pain meant little to her. She was worried about David. "I have to, Kat, you have to see that. If he isn't stopped now, he will become too powerful. The

Clan of the Black Rings will rise, and then none of the dead will stay dead. All will come back to serve him."

She stared at both her grandfather and Kyoshi. They were talking about David as if he were some evil person. She wouldn't let them do it. How could Grandfather think such things? And Kyoshi was talking about his only son!

Kat jumped across the table and reached for the sword before her grandfather could pull it away. Kyoshi was fast and grabbed her before she could touch the sword, but her wet clothes were slippery and he didn't get a good hold on her. Kat stretched her hand for the blade of the wooden sword. Kyoshi and Grandfather tried to haul her away, but she twisted and turned her body until she could almost touch it.

And then she did.

Kat felt a surge of electricity pass though her, but it didn't hurt. A brilliant light flashed and she felt as if someone was running a giant vacuum cleaner over her as her skin seemed to stretch. Her stomach turned like she was on an upside down roller coaster.

Then the world went gray...dark gray.

CHAPTER TEN
A Covering of Armor

Kat tried to focus, but everything was spinning. Shapes began to form and she could see moving figures. It was like watching a film in black and white on a gray screen. The figures were samurai warriors fighting each other. Gradually colors started to appear, but they were covered by the gray fog. She saw the red armor of a warrior that led the way. He easily fought off his attackers, then looked towards her. He charged at her, and Kat realized she couldn't move. He kept coming towards her. It was Toho! She recognized him from the painting. He was large, and his armor was not just red from the metal, but from blood. He stood in front of her and raised his sword. It was reddish gold and she knew it was the Heavensblade. He then flipped it so it rested on his arm and pushed it towards Kat, who found herself reaching for the sword. Kat couldn't help herself.

When she looked down and saw the sword guard, she saw a hand holding the handle. It was encased in a glove, a red glove with metal strips on top of the fingers. She saw the hand move. She made the hand move. It was her hand.

Kat looked around. The gray mist was fading. She was still in the kitchen, and could make out two shadowy figures rising off the floor. Kat backed away, unsure of what to do. The figures approached her, and Kat staggered out the open door.

Kat heard voices from the two shadowy figures. She kept backing away and slipped to the ground. Kat looked into the mist and made out the faces of the two shadows. Their voices, which had sounded far away, now seemed to be very close.

The first shadow voice asked her, "What

have you done?"

She knew this was the voice of the man who said he was her father. It was Kyoshi.

Kat felt confused. Now she saw Kyoshi and Grandfather, although they were still surrounded by a slight mist. The sky was dark and the rain was still falling, yet she could see more stars than she ever saw before.

"Kat! Can you hear me?" It was Grandfather.

"I hear you." She looked down and saw that she was covered in red armor. Her hand went up to her head and she felt a helmet.

Her grandfather stepped closer. "Relax, Kat. Relax like I taught you. Breathe deeply and push everything out of your head for a moment."

Kat did as instructed. She closed her eyes and slowly breathed in and out, letting her body relax until she could feel her heartbeat returning to normal. When Kat opened her eyes, she had hoped that everything would be normal again, but she was still in the world of gray.

Kat gazed at Grandfather. "This armor? Is this the armor of Toho?"

Grandfather touched her. "It must be. But I cannot see it. To me, you still look like my young granddaughter holding a wooden sword."

Kat looked again at the armor she was wearing. "That's impossible! I have this red armor on! And the sword–it's metal, not wood! Why did this happen to me and not David?"

Grandfather thought for a moment. "You both have blood of Toho and Hiro in you. It must be the rings that

David is wearing. They brought out the Hiro side."

Kyoshi stepped towards them "We don't have time. Kat, you have to get ready."

"Ready for what?" she asked.

Kyoshi pointed towards the path that led to the dojo. "For David."

Kat turned to look at the path. "David? Why?"

Kyoshi grabbed Kat's shoulders and spun her around to face him. "He is going to come after you. He knows you have the sword of Toho. He can sense it. In order to gain all the power he can, he must take your sword. He must take the Heavensblade."

Kat threw the sword to the ground. "He can have it!"

Kyoshi picked up the sword. To him, it was wood, but Kat could see the reddish gold shining in the starlight. "The sword is not all he will want, Kat. He wants you to die."

"But why? Why would David do that?" Kat

started to cry.

Kyoshi gently wiped away Kat's tears. "Because that is no longer David. It is Hiro. You have to remember that. When David put those rings on, he turned away from Toho and embraced Hiro."

Kat sniffed. She wiped her face, but the rough glove dug into her cheek. Kat didn't want any part of this. It didn't seem real before, but now it was all too real.

She looked at the sword Kyoshi held out for her and asked him, "Why don't you take the sword?"

Kyoshi didn't move. "I can't. Once someone has taken up the katana of Toho or Hiro, that person's hold over it can only be released..." he hesitated, "...it can only be released by death."

He pushed the sword toward Kat again.

She opened her hand and took it. It seemed much heavier now.

Kyoshi gazed at the path to the dojo. "The circle is complete. Now the samurai of the past will seek out their leader, Hiro, and join him. They will make a new army of the dead." Turning back towards the others, Kyoshi motioned to Grandfather. "Father, find us some weapons. Kat will make her stand here, but we will join her. Maybe the three of us will have a chance."

Grandfather hurried as fast as he could into the house while Kat and Kyoshi waited to see when David would come down the path.

Kat turned and looked at the man next to her. Kyoshi stepped in front of her as if to protect her. Kat wanted to hide behind him, but she knew that whatever was going to happen, how it turned out was going to be up to her. She thought about asking Kyoshi something that she had wanted to ask from the moment he arrived, but she wasn't sure this was the right time for it.

"Why did you leave us?" Kat was surprised that she said this out loud.

Kyoshi turned towards her. He glanced at her, but kept his eyes on the path.

"I wish I had more time to explain, Katherine." He sighed. "After your mother's death, I wanted revenge. The Clan of the Black Rings is involved in crime all over the world, and I wanted to hurt them because of what they did to your mother. That revenge was all I had in my life at that time."

Kat looked at him with hope. "So, you were some kind of cop or something?"

Now Kyoshi gave her his full attention. "No, Kat, I wasn't." He looked down. "I did some bad things, things that were not honorable. I am not proud of this. I went to my father and asked him to take my children and start a new life and to never try to contact me."

"But didn't you want to know where we were? Didn't you want to come back?"

Kyoshi faced the path again. "If I had known where you were, then I could have told the Black Rings if they found me. No man, no matter how he tried, can resist torture."

"But they never found you."

Kyoshi glanced back at Kat. "They found me. At the time, I wished I had known where you were so I could have told them to end the pain." He turned back towards the path.

Kat looked at the back of her father's head, surprised she wasn't mad. She realized that she understood what he must have gone through.

She looked down at the armor that covered her. It all seemed so unreal. Her whole life had been turned upside down. Her grandfather hid so much from her and she always thought that they shared everything. Her brother was no longer her brother, if she believed what Grandfather

said and the man in front of her was a father she never knew she had.

Kat wished that it was yesterday. She wanted to go back to a normal dull day when she worried about what to wear to school, what boy said what things about her, and dealing with homework.

She jumped when she heard the clanging of swords.

It was Grandfather who returned with two swords. He gave one to Kyoshi. "They are good swords," he said, "but no match for Hiro."

Kyoshi balanced the sword in his hand. "They will have to do."

Kat watched as Kyoshi practiced with his sword. His movements were quick. She was shocked at how fast and smooth he was. She had always thought that Grandfather was good with a sword, but he wasn't nearly as good at Kyoshi.

She saw Kyoshi stop. Kat looked where her father was looking, and saw that David was coming.

CHAPTER ELEVEN
The Vision of Toho

It was David, but he was in the armor of Hiro. Her brother walked straight ahead and stared directly at Kat. That made her feel uneasy.

Kyoshi stepped up, holding his sword with both hands in front of him. "Do you know who I am?"

David looked away from Kat. "Yes, I know. It doesn't matter."

With no hesitation, David swung his sword at Kyoshi. Kyoshi deflected the swing, but before he could attack David, the black sword of Hiro swung again and Kyoshi was pushed back. David was too strong for him.

Each time David's blade crossed Kyoshi's it knocked him back.

David finally held the black sword with both hands and swung hard, breaking Kyoshi's sword in half. Kyoshi dropped to his knees from the force, and David raised the black sword to deliver a killing blow.

Grandfather stepped in and deflected David's blow with his sword, but the black blade hit Kyoshi's shoulder. Kyoshi cried out as David's sword cut his arm deeply. Grandfather tried to raise his sword again, but David knocked Grandfather to the ground with the back of his hand.

David came straight for Kat.

She raised her sword.

David swung his sword with both hands. Kat was shocked at how strong he was. Each time he swung at her and she blocked him, it knocked her back a few steps. Kat was afraid. She didn't stand a chance. David kept after her and she was growing weaker. Kat didn't know what to do. She would have dropped the sword and ran, but David never gave her the chance. He just kept coming. Then he swung again and her sword flew out of her hands.

David raised his sword and when Kat looked into his eyes, she knew the person she was fighting was no longer David. It was Hiro, and he was going to strike her with everything he had.

Suddenly David stumbled forward, and Kat saw that Grandfather had delivered a flying kick into his back. The kick knocked David to the ground, but he quickly recovered and turned towards Grandfather. Kat watched as David slashed at Grandfather, again and again, each blow pushing him back.

"Kat, pick up the sword!" Kat saw Kyoshi crawling towards her. "Pick it up!"

Kat picked up the sword. She looked at Kyoshi. "Father! What do I do?"

Kyoshi struggled to his feet. "Reach into yourself, Kat. Let yourself go. The sword is the power. Let it flow inside of you. The spirit of the samurai will guide you, but you have to let it. Use your training, but let the spirit come from the sword."

Kat stared at the katana of Toho, then closed her eyes and relaxed. As she did, she saw a vision. It was Toho standing on a bloodied battlefield, his hands clasped around hers on the sword. He looked at her and she heard him say, "You are my blood. My spirit and the spirit of all that followed me now join you. You must lead us, all of us."

Kat opened her eyes. The sword felt light, as if it were part of her. She looked over to her grandfather. He was on the ground as David knocked his sword away.

"David!" she yelled.

David stopped and looked towards Kat.

"The Heavensblade will be mine," he said as he walked towards her.

Kat stood her ground. She raised the sword with both hands, and this time she felt ready.

David didn't slow down and swung his blade while coming towards her. Kat blocked it and realized that this time David's strength didn't knock her back. She blocked another blow, and then she swung her sword, twisted around, and delivered another blow. Her sword hit David on his side and he cried out. Kat saw blood run red down David's black armor.

David rushed her, but Kat moved aside and delivered another blow. She thought that this was a lot like their practice sessions. David was stronger, but he rushed his fighting. She was quicker, so she used that to her advantage. The swords may have been magical, and both of them may have been fed speed and power by the spirits, but now Kat understood that it was still David and Kat who were fighting. Toho and Hiro were only the weapons.

Kat found herself gaining strength even as David's

blows grew weaker. The sword of Toho moved almost with her thoughts alone, and she began to press her attack. She forced David back, but she never forgot that he was still the stronger, and by attacking him she was playing to his strengths. Kat retreated a little so David could push his attack more.

David sensed that he was wearing Kat down. She was backing up each time he delivered a blow, so he believed he had to press the attack even more. His swings became wilder as he put all of his strength into each swipe. He kept after his sister, who now was just trying to block his blows.

Kat dropped her guard a little as David raised his sword to deliver a powerful blow with both hands. She had to time her next move just right.

David stepped forward as he swung at her with all of his strength, but Kat also moved forward instead of stepping back. She put her foot between David's feet and let the momentum of David's swing carry him past her. Kat was surprised that David fell for the same move she had used on him so many times before. As he stumbled, Kat twisted and swung her blade and hit David on the back.

David landed on the ground hard and his sword fell

out of his hand. Kat rushed over and raised her sword. She told herself that this was not David any longer but Hiro. That she couldn't stop now.

As she was about to bring her sword down, David looked at her and held his hand up. "Kat, it's me. David."

Kat stopped. It was David! Was Hiro gone? She

lowered her sword. David started to get up. He looked around. "What happened? I don't remember anything."

Kat sighed. How could she explain this to David? She looked first at Kyoshi, blood pooling from his arm and then at Grandfather lying on the ground. He was not moving.

Kat stared at Grandfather, afraid to go any closer, then she heard Kyoshi yell. She turned around and saw that David had retrieved the sword of Hiro. He was raising his sword against her! Kat managed to block the blow, but it knocked her to the ground. She rolled quickly to her knees, holding her sword so she could stop David's next strike.

David saw how quickly Kat recovered. Instead of coming after her, he turned around and ran. Kat got up and thought about pursuing him, but instead she ran to her grandfather.

Kyoshi staggered next to her. "He's badly hurt. He needs to get to the hospital."

Kat looked towards the woods where David had run. "What do I do?"

Kyoshi looked into her eyes. "Family comes first."

Kat agreed.

CHAPTER TWELVE
Acceptance of All Things

In Grandfather's hospital room, Kat sat next to Kyoshi. Even though she hadn't known her father for very long, she was beginning to feel more comfortable around him. Kyoshi's arm was in a sling, but he refused any other treatment so that he could sit with his father. Kat looked at the case next to her feet. It held her sword and she thought that from now on she would have to make sure it was always near.

Grandfather had been awake for a little while, but now he was tiring. He and Kyoshi had talked, but it was mostly in whispers so Kat couldn't hear what they said.

"Kat," Grandfather finally called to her weakly.

"Come closer."

Kat leaned in as Kyoshi backed away. Grandfather stroked her hair. "I am so proud of you, Kat. You proved that you are true Toho clan."

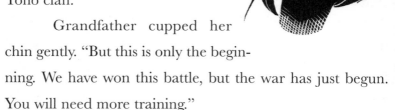

Grandfather cupped her chin gently. "But this is only the beginning. We have won this battle, but the war has just begun. You will need more training."

Kat smiled. "You have to get well first, Grandfather."

Grandfather shook his head. "No, Kat, you need more training than I can give you. You need a Master, someone who is much more skilled than I in the arts."

Grandfather raised his hand and pointed towards Kyoshi. "You need your father."

Kyoshi bowed. "I will be honored, Katherine, if you will let me train you." He looked away before softly adding, "And if you would let me be part of your life."

Kat stepped in front of Kyoshi. "I will, but only on one condition."

Kyoshi raised an eyebrow, wondering what the condition could be.

Kat smiled. "You have to let me call you Dad. Father is so formal."

Kyoshi nodded and then turned away. Kat could tell he didn't know what to say. But if she could see his face, she would have seen the glistening tear as the light from the morning sun touched his face.

THE END

ABOUT THE WRITER

Gary Reed is the former publisher of Caliber Comics and writer of hundreds of comics and books.

His graphic novel projects include *DRACULA* and *FRANKENSTEIN* from Penguin Books, and *SAINT GERMAINE* and *DEADWORLD* from Image Comics.

Gary lives in the Detroit/Ann Arbor area and in additon to being a freelance writer, he also teaches biology at several local community colleges.

ABOUT
THE ARTIST

Rick Hoberg was born in Texas and raised in California. He grew up loving illustrated books, comics and cartoons. Rick has had a terrific career drawing comic books (*BATMAN, JUSTICE LEAGUE, STAR WARS*) and contributing storyboards to animated television shows and films (*X-MEN, SPIDER-MAN, THE LAND BEFORE TIME*). Rick is pleased to finally add book illustrator to his list of accomplishments.

ACKNOWLEDGEMENTS:

Gary thanks Steve Jones and his daughters, Alison and Erica, for reading the story before it was a story.

Rick would like to give his thanks to Patrick and Shannon at Komikwerks for the guidance, and to Glenn Koening, Paul Hoberg, Anna and Joe Mattaino, Chris Hoberg, Paula Williams, Owen Souther, Vince Mattaino, Strider, Henry, and Arwen for all the love.

Creative Direction and Editor: Shannon Eric Denton
Book Design and Production: Patrick Coyle

Special thanks to John Helfers, Aron Lusen, and Hope Aguilar.

The publishers wish to thank Dakota, Katherine, Kristen, and Wyatt for their continued support and inspiration, and Byron Preiss for his belief in our vision.

The text type for this book is set in Baskerville.
The display type is Seven Swordsmen.
The illustrations are pen, brush, and ink.

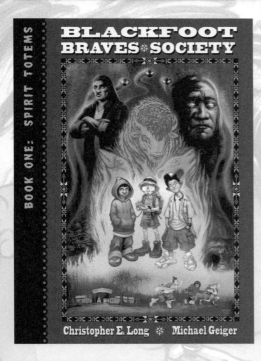

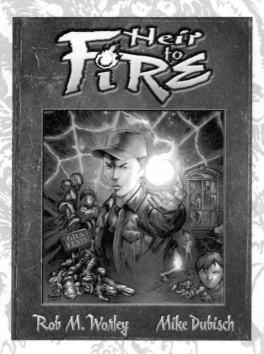